JOANIE

Cartoons for New Children

JOANIE

Cartoons for New Children

A Doonesbury Book

By

Garry Trudeau

With an Afterword for Parents and Teachers
By Nora Ephron

Sheed and Ward, Inc.
Subsidiary of Universal Press Syndicate

The "Cartoons for New Children Series"
is edited by Garry Trudeau, creator of
"Doonesbury." Future selections will
include the contributions of a number of other
distinguished cartoonists and illustrators
whose work is well-known to newspaper
audiences.

Already released is:
What Is God's Area Code?
A Kelly-Duke Book by Jack Moore

"Doonesbury" is distributed internationally by
UNIVERSAL PRESS SYNDICATE

ISBN: 0-8362-0600-2 (hardbound)
ISBN: 0-8362-0581-2 (paperback)

Library of Congress Catalog Card Number 74-1543

To Lynton

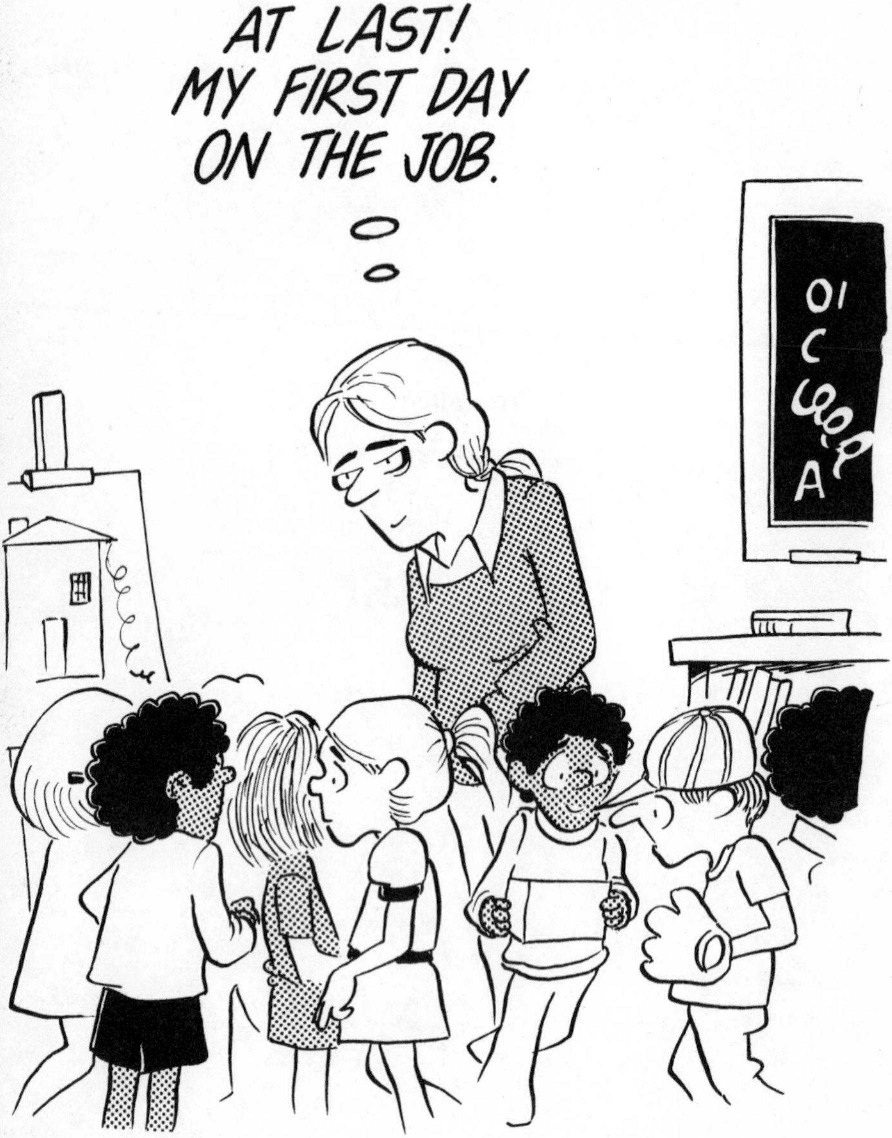
AT LAST!
MY FIRST DAY
ON THE JOB.

HEY, PEOPLE, I'VE GOT AN IDEA! LET'S FIND OUT WHAT YOU ALL WANT TO BE WHEN YOU GROW UP! FIRST, THE *BOYS!*

11

GROWING UP TO BE A MOMMY IS ONE OF THE MOST WONDERFUL THINGS A LITTLE GIRL CAN WANT TO DO. *BUT* — THERE ARE OTHER THINGS IN LIFE SHE CAN DO AS WELL.. !

FOR INSTANCE, SHE CAN WORK HER HEAD OFF AND SHOW ALL THOSE ARROGANT BOYS THAT SHE'S JUST AS CAPABLE AND INTELLIGENT AS ANY LITTLE STUD AROUND!!

HAVE YOU BEEN DOWN TO VISIT JOANIE AT THE DAY CARE CENTER YET?
NO... HOW'S HER NEW JOB GOING?

OKAY, I GUESS — SHE'S BEEN ADMINISTERING CONSCIOUSNESS RAISING SESSIONS TO THE GIRLS...

TERRIFIC!

WELL, I DON'T KNOW — JOANIE MAY BE ASKING TOO MUCH OF LITTLE GIRLS OF THAT AGE..

NONSENSE! I'M SURE THAT SHE'S HANDLING IT BEAUTIFULLY.

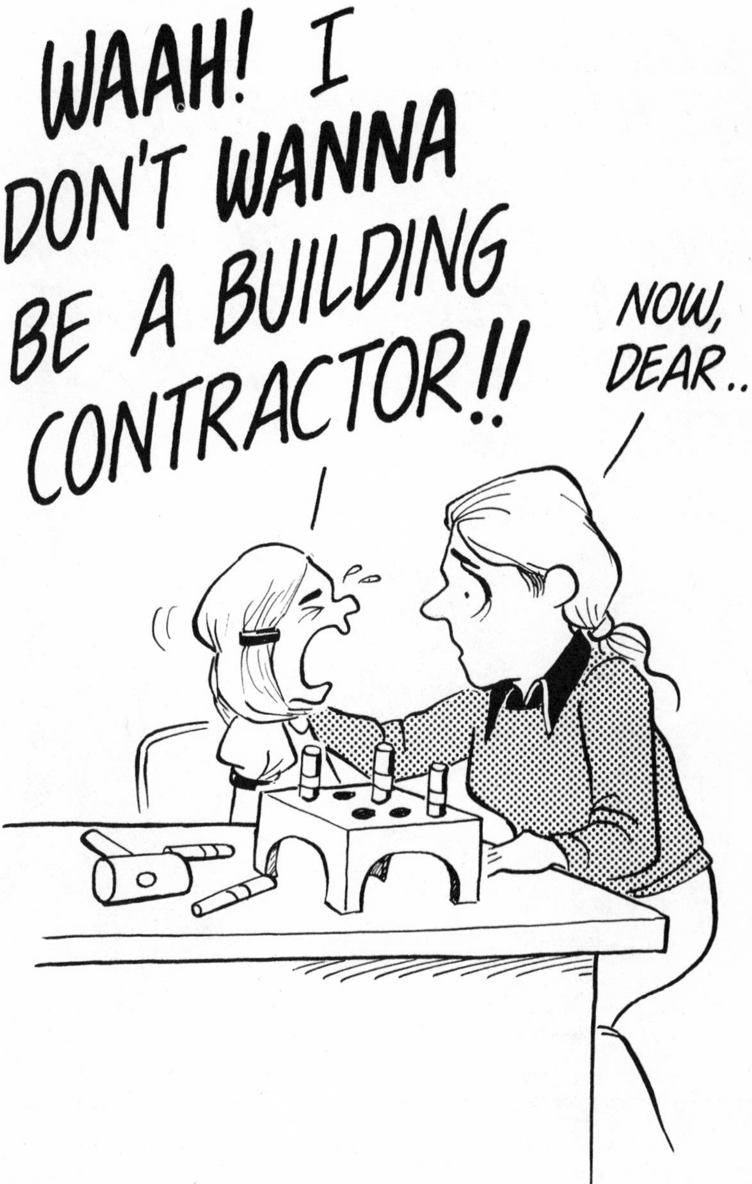
WAAH! I DON'T WANNA BE A BUILDING CONTRACTOR!!
NOW, DEAR..

MS. CAUCUS, WE BOYS HAVE BEEN NOTICING A BIG CHANGE IN THE GIRLS LATELY. THEY'VE BEEN ACTING LIKE BOYS!
WELL, DEAR, I'M NOT SURE YOU BOYS ARE BEING QUITE FAIR..

A GREAT LADY, SIMONE DE BEAUVOIR, ONCE SAID THAT THERE ARE TWO KINDS OF PEOPLE — HUMAN BEINGS AND WOMEN. BUT WHEN WOMEN START ACTING LIKE HUMAN BEINGS, THEY ARE ACCUSED OF TRYING TO BE LIKE MEN.

SIMONE DE BEAUVOIR'S GOT YOUR NUMBER, SLIM.

32

33

MOMMY GOES INTO THE HOSPITAL TODAY. I GUESS I BETTER START THINKING POSITIVELY ABOUT MY NEWEST SIBLING..

GOOD IDEA, DEAR!

ALSO, IT'S MORE "IN" TO BE A FEMALE THAN A MALE THESE DAYS! MUCH MORE FASHIONABLE.
IT IS?
SURE!

41

42

43

I DROPPED BY THE DAY CARE CENTER THIS MORNING.
OH? HOW'S JOANIE DOING?

OKAY, I GUESS.. ALL THE LITTLE GIRLS DOWN THERE HAVE A NEW IDOL.
WHO'S THAT?

48

49

53

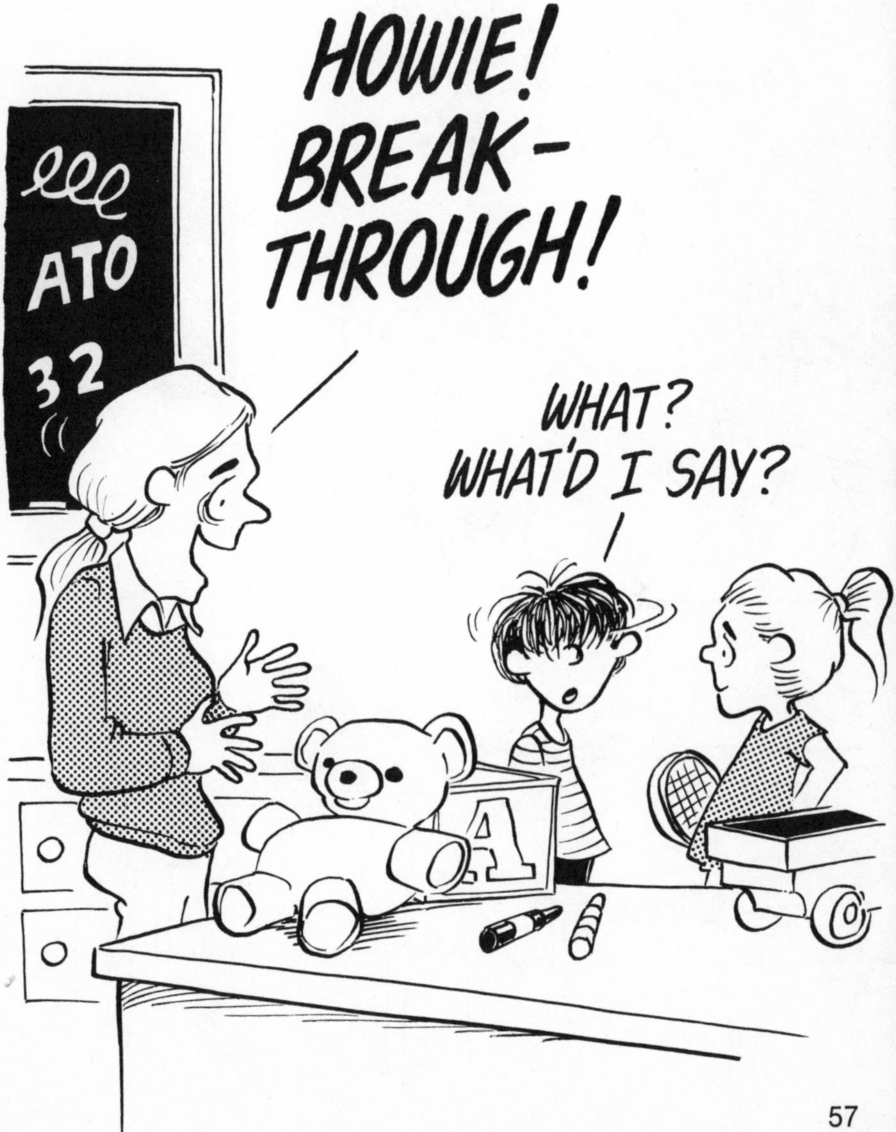
HOWIE! BREAK-THROUGH!
WHAT? WHAT'D I SAY?
ATO
32
A

WHO'S THIS?.. ZONKER? HI, KIDDO– IT'S JOANIE. SAY, WHO'S MAKING DINNER TONIGHT? DO YOU KNOW?..
DOUBLE FAULT!
HEE! HEE!
OL
4+7

59

WHAT?.. WELL, I PROMISED LISA I'D HELP HER STRING HER RACQUET.. IT MEANS A LOT TO HER, SO..
HEE! HEE!
WHEE!
HA!
OL
4+2

61

63

71

WHAT DO YOU MEAN, MY EGGS AREN'T READY!? HOW LONG DOES IT TAKE TO COOK TWO LOUSY EGGS?! **HUH?!**

I'VE GOT A LONG DAY AHEAD OF ME, SO HURRY UP WITH THOSE EGGS BEFORE I LOSE MY TEMPER!

I DON'T KNOW WHAT YOU'RE TALKING ABOUT MR. ALLEN. I HAVE NOT BEEN "FEEDING MARY A LOT OF SUB-VERSIVE POPPYCOCK"!
l 4 B
9
6

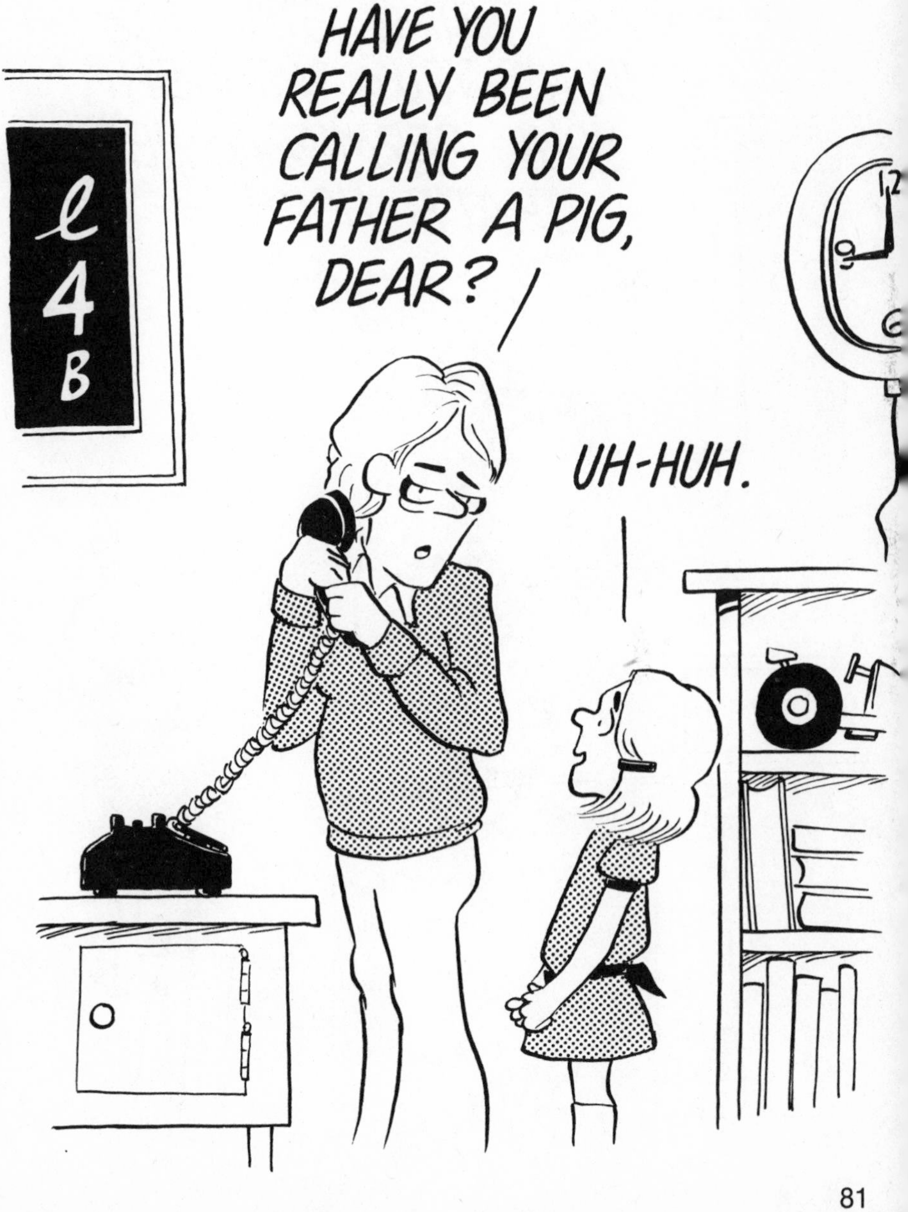
HAVE YOU REALLY BEEN CALLING YOUR FATHER A PIG, DEAR?
UH-HUH.

83

Afterword for Parents and Teachers

By Nora Ephron

I live in a city that has only a few major failings—and one of them is that there are no newspapers that carry "Doonesbury" in their comics sections. So I came late to Garry Trudeau and his characters, heard about them at a party in Washington, when a woman friend told me all about someone named Joanie Caucus. Ms. Caucus. I sat through the conversation smiling patiently, humoring my friend, because I did not believe her. Joanie Caucus, she told me, was funny. Genuinely funny. It seemed to me that the likelihood of that was next to impossible. I should point out that I am not one of those who believe that there is nothing to laugh at about the women's movement; in fact, there is plenty to laugh about without in any way putting down the movement, and I become downright irritable when I read lengthy feminist tracts justifying the women's movement's lack of a sense of humor. "How can we laugh when we're so oppressed?" That kind of thing. It seems to me that the exact opposite is true: how can we *not* laugh when we're so oppressed. In spite of what I feel about the women's movement, in spite of the huge role it has played in my life, there are aspects of it that are just plain funny. Not at the time. I have to say that. But afterward, when I think that I spent days, weeks even, discussing who was going to sort the socks, *his* socks—well, you get the picture.

In any case, the women's movement has spawned very little humor—much less any humor that amuses rhe. And Joanie Caucus hardly seemed a likely candidate; she was, after all, the creation of a man. Then I started reading "Doonesbury," and there was Joanie, the runaway wife, the day-care center supervisor, the law school applicant, the newly-single woman coping with passes from a hip priest with hot tickets to a Jeb Magruder concert, and I began to roar.

There is nothing more hopeless than attempting to explain why something is funny. Once, in the course of a checkered newspaper career, I had to read excerpts from a college thesis on humor by Johnny Carson; he took a series of absolutely hilarious jokes by Jack Benny and Fred Allen and rendered them utterly stultifying with his long-winded analyses of what made them work. I don't want to do that to Joanie. For one thing, I am a little in love with her. For another, I have no idea why she is funny. I just know she kills me. And I think about her all the time. It's not just that I know women like her and that I'm a little like her myself. It's not just that my friends constantly tell me stories about trying to bring the movement to their children, stories that are remarkably like the episodes in this book. It's also that there is something about what she looks like and the way she behaves— so downtrodden and yet plucky, so saggy and yet upright, so droopy-eyed and yet wide awake, so pessimistic and yet deep-down slyly sure that she's on the right track. I don't want to take this too seriously, but she seems such a perfect, sympathetic mirror-image of all of us who are trying to make sense out of the contradictions, trying to assimilate all the new information and ideas and theories into our messy lives and minds. It's not easy, folks—and I love that Joanie makes it look so hard. It's occasionally absurd and ridiculous—and I love that she makes it look so funny. It seems to me that this book provides a perfect, abso-

lutely painless way for parents to introduce some of these ideas to
their children.

I got to the end of this lovely book, to the strip where Joanie
tells Mary that her parents are withdrawing her from the day-care
center: Joanie with her false bravado, her "scoot" to cover her
feelings. And Mary, who is smarter than the rest of us, knows
that it is she who must offer the reassurance. "Hang in there,
sister!" she says. And Joanie's mouth snakes upward, in that de-
liciously wicked way it tends to. "I will, dear," she says.

God, it's wonderful.

ALLIGATOR BOOK